The Firefighter

Adaptation of the animated series: Sarah Margaret Johanson
Illustrations: Eric Sévigny, based on the animated series

chouette

"It's almost time for our special visitor," Miss Martin said.
"Everyone sit down, please."
Excitedly, Caillou and the other children sat down.
Caillou was wearing a special hat today for their visitor.
"Leo, come and sit over here," Caillou said.
"Okay! Thanks, Caillou."

"Who knows what a smoke detector is?" Miss Martin asked. "A smoke detector tells us if there's smoke in the air. And why is this important to know?"
"Because if there's smoke that means there's a fire somewhere," Jason called out.
"Right! We have a smoke detector in our classroom. Can you find it?"
The children looked all around.

"I'll give you a hint," Miss Martin said. "Smoke rises, so where should a smoke detector be?"

Everyone looked up.

"There it is!"

"I see it, too. It's on the ceiling!" Caillou said.

"Well done! And look, our visitor is here. Say good morning to our fire chief."

"Hello. I see we already have some firefighters in the class. I count four firefighter hats," the fire chief said. Caillou and Leo giggled, because Caillou was one of the firefighters with his special hat.

"Now, fires don't happen very often if everyone is careful," the fire chief explained. "But a fire can be dangerous, so we all need to know what to do."

"That's why today we'll test the alarm and practice what to do if there's a fire in the school. Does anyone know what that's called?"
"A fire drill," Caillou said.
"Right! So whenever you hear the alarm, you should stop what you're doing and leave the building right away."

"Would you like to hear how loud the alarm is?"
the fire chief asked.
"Yeah!" everyone said.
"Get ready, here it comes," Miss Martin warned.
The alarm gave a short but very, very loud blast.
"Was that loud enough for you?" the chief laughed.

"So we've heard the alarm and now we need to get organized and get outside quickly," the chief said. "We also need to be quiet so that if someone is telling us what to do, we can all hear it," Miss Martin said. "Everyone ready?"

"Okay, Leo, give me your hand. Everyone hold hands and form a line," the fire chief instructed.
The class quietly went outside to the playground. They were surprised to see a fire truck waiting outside.
"Wow! Look at that!"
"Cool!"

"Good work, everybody!" the fire chief said. "Oh, and here comes my friend, Sparky. Say hello to our new friends."
"Woof, woof," Sparky greeted the children.
Everyone crowded around to pet and say hello to Sparky.
"He's cute."
"Now, who would like to sit in the fire truck?" asked the fire chief.

"Me, please! Me, please," Leo and Caillou answered.
"Okay, get ready because this siren is even louder. It has to tell all the cars on the road to pull over and let the fire truck through," the fire chief explained. "Ready? Caillou pull that cord over there."
"B-L-A-R-E!" A very loud siren sounded.

"I'm going to be a firefighter when I grow up," Caillou exclaimed.
"Well, we'd be very happy to have you on the team," the fire chief said, helping both boys down off the truck.
"I'm going to be a firefighter when I grow up, too," Leo said.
Caillou thought that he and his best friend Leo would make a great firefighting team.

Text: adaptation by Sarah Margaret Johanson of the animated series CAILLOU, produced by DHX Media Inc.

Original scenario written by Mary Mackay-Smith
Original episode #304: Caillou The Firefighter
Illustrations: Eric Sévigny, based on the animated series CAILLOU.
Art Direction: Monique Dupras

We acknowledge the financial support of the Government of Canada through the Canada Book Fund for our publishing activities.

Canadian Heritage Patrimoine canadien

We acknowledge the support of the Ministry of Culture and Communications of Quebec and SODEC for the publication and promotion of this book.

SODEC Québec

Bibliothèque et Archives nationales du Québec and Library and Archives Canada cataloguing in publication

Johanson, Sarah Margaret, 1968-
Caillou: the firefighter
(Playtime)
To be accompanied by a poster.
For children aged 3 and up.

ISBN 978-2-89450-861-9

1. Fire prevention - Juvenile literature. 2. Fire drills - Juvenile literature. 3. Fire fighters - Juvenile literature. I. Sévigny, Éric. II. Title. III. Title: Firefighter. IV. Series: Playtime (Montréal, Québec).

TH9148.J63 2013 j628.9'2 C2012-941686-X

Printed in Shenzhen, China
10 9 8 7 6 5 4 3 CHO1891 JUL2013